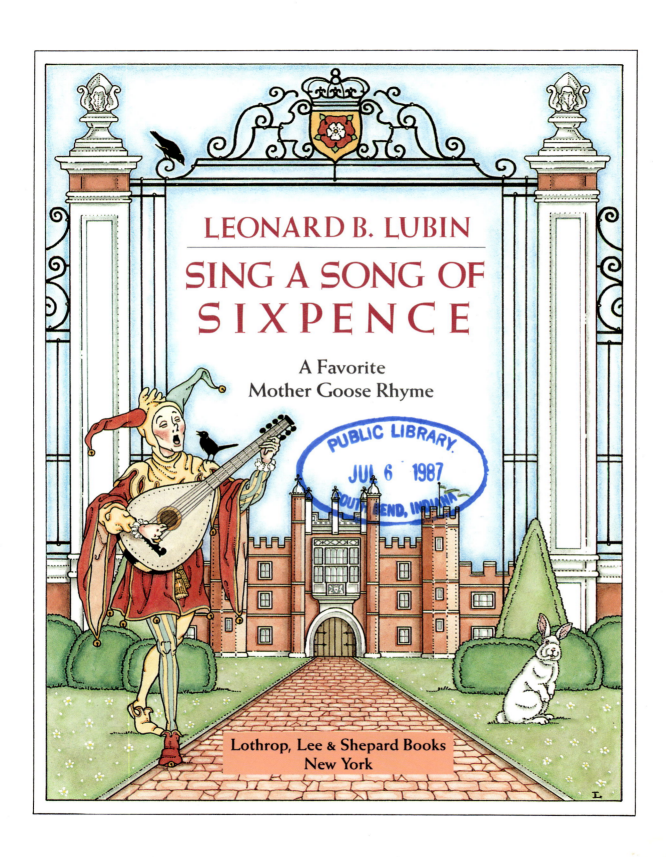

LEONARD B. LUBIN

SING A SONG OF
SIXPENCE

A Favorite
Mother Goose Rhyme

Lothrop, Lee & Shepard Books
New York

To Jane Peck and Marty White

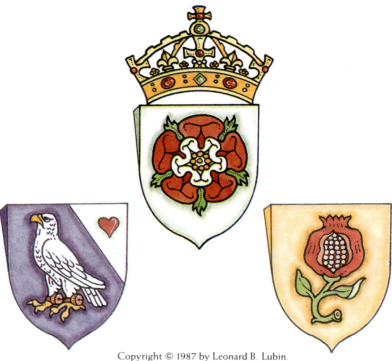

First Edition   1 2 3 4 5 6 7 8 9 10

Library of Congress Cataloging in Publication Data
Sing a song of sixpence.
Summary: An illustrated version, set in the time of Henry VIII, of the traditional
rhyme about the four-and-twenty blackbirds baked in a pie.
1. Nursery rhymes. 2. Children's poetry. [1. Nursery rhymes] I. Lubin, Leonard
B., ill. PZ8.3.S614 1987   387'.8   86-10337
ISBN 0-688-00544-6
ISBN 0-688-00545-4 (lib. bdg.)

ING A SONG OF SIXPENCE,

like many Mother Goose rhymes, is based on historical fact. This jingle portrays events in the life of Henry VIII (1491–1547), who began his reign as king of England in 1509, when he was eighteen years old. The lines refer to his seizure of Church revenues and lands, his insistence on a divorce from Katherine of Aragon, and his involvement with and ultimate disposal of Anne Boleyn.

The sixpence and rye represent the money and rich grainfields that were confiscated from the Church to become Henry's possessions. The pie (which figures similarly in the rhyme "Little Jack Horner") was presented to Henry by the abbot of Newstead. The abbot hoped to ingratiate himself with the king by offering him a pastry shell that contained four and twenty deeds of title to choice Church properties. The singing blackbirds represent a black-robed monk for each of the deeds. The abbot's gift pleased the greedy king, who added the booty to other wealth accumulated in his "counting-house."

Meanwhile, Queen Katherine, reassured by her Spanish relatives that the Church would not allow Henry to divorce her, sat in her parlor eating "bread" (Henry's slights and indignities) and "honey" (the belief that Spain and the Church would somehow preserve her marriage).

The "maid," Anne Boleyn, who for a time was maid-in-waiting to the queen, returned from a visit to France and caught the king's fancy with her continental manners and French clothes. According to legend, Henry first took notice of Anne Boleyn in the gardens of Whitehall Palace. Anne was courted, Katherine divorced, and Henry married his "maid."

Anne's day in the sun didn't last, however. Among the many things she did to displease Henry was to bear him a girl child, whom they named Elizabeth. Another "blackbird," in the person of the royal headsman, eventually relieved Anne of not just her nose, but her entire head.

The rest, as they say, is history.

L. B. L.

I

Sing a song of sixpence,
A pocket full of rye;
Four and twenty blackbirds
Baked in a pie.

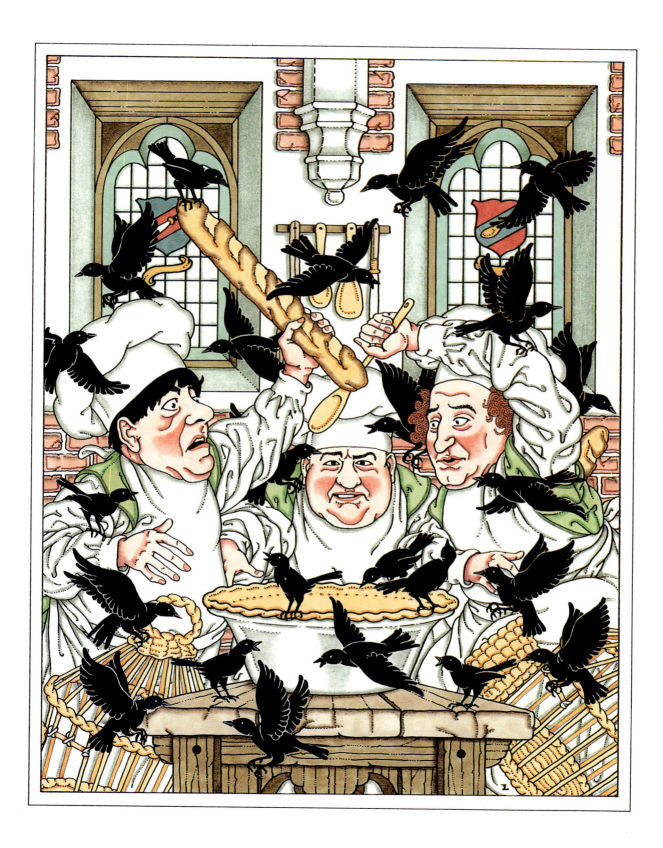

II

When the pie was open'd,
The birds began to sing;
Was not that a dainty dish
To set before the king?

III

The king was in the counting-house,
Counting out his money;
The queen was in the parlor,
Eating bread and honey.

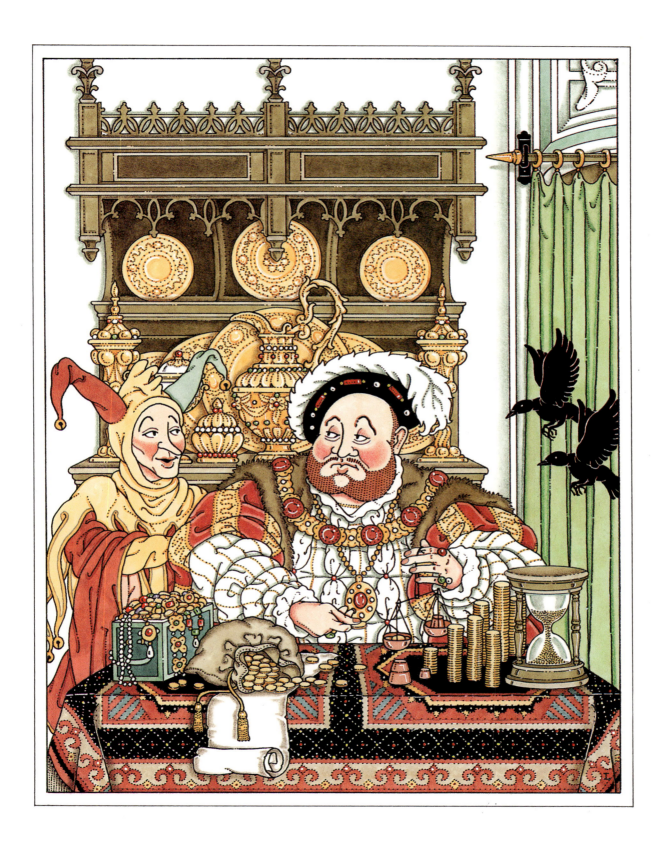

IV

The maid was in the garden,
Hanging out the clothes;
Down came a blackbird,
And pecked off her nose.